Waggers

by

Philemon Sturges

illustrated by

Jim Ishikawa

DUTTON CHILDREN'S BOOKS · NEW YORK

To Doris and Jack, who first told me this tale,
and to Dr. Jay, who knows more about waggers than I care to
P.S.

To my brother, Hideto
J.I.

Text copyright © 2005 by Philemon Sturges
Illustrations copyright © 2005 by Jim Ishikawa

Library of Congress Cataloging-in-Publication Data
Sturges, Philemon.
Waggers/by Philemon Sturges; illustrated by Jim Ishikawa.—1st ed.
p. cm.
Summary: This rhyming story reveals the real reason why dogs always sniff each other when they meet.
ISBN 0-525-47116-2
[1. Dogs—Fiction. 2. Cats—Fiction. 3. Humorous stories. 4. Stories in rhyme.] I. Ishikawa, Jim, ill. II. Title.
PZ8.3.S9227Wag 2005
[E]—dc22
2004011126

Published in the United States by Dutton Children's Books,
a division of Penguin Young Readers Group
345 Hudson Street, New York, New York 10014
www.penguin.com

Manufactured in China
First Edition
1 3 5 7 9 10 8 6 4 2

Tell me, sir, please tell me, ma'am,
and you as well, my child,
have you ever paused to wonder,
as you looked away and smiled,
when a doggy meets another one,
why they never just pass by?
There's a reason for their antics,
and this tale will tell you why.

The doggies held a meeting.
They came from near and far.
Some came by motorcycle,
and some by motorcar.

A few dogs came by chopper,
a few by aeroplane.
And one, I'm told, was very bold
and took the morning train.

The Doggy Lodge was far away.
The time was long ago.
They gathered to discuss the Cat,
their ancient, dreaded foe.

Each doggy went inside the hall.
Each doggy signed the book.

Each removed its wagger
and hung it on a hook.

The meeting was important.
The subject? It was that:
The world would be much better
if Dog got rid of Cat.

The dogs said, "Cats are heartless.
They spit and scratch and hiss."

"One woof and, my, their backs arch high.
We shan't put up with this!"

"With cats around, the house smells bad:
old litter, rotting rat.
When Master comes, they preen and purr,
and *Kitty* gets the pat!"

A cat learned of the meeting
and thought she'd try to spy.
Perhaps she might discover
the deep-down reason why...

kindly, well-dressed humans,
who love a soothing purr,
tolerate those useless bags
of flea-infested fur!

Dogs drool and pant and slobber.
They race around the park.
They jump and bounce and gnaw and dig

and never cease to bark.

Cat made herself a doggy suit,
complete with doggy tail.
She walked boldly to the meeting

and hung it on a nail.

Top Dog stood and shouted:
"All in favor, please bark 'AYE.'
Let every cat be rounded up
for cat and kitty pie!"

That cat, as you can understand,
was filled with dread and fear.
She vowed to take some action
lest Catdom's end be near.

So before the vote was taken,
she did a deed most dire.
With brave determination,
she stood and hollered,

Each doggy leaped in horror
and, without a second look,
grabbed whichever wagger
was on the nearest hook.

Dogs ran in all directions.
Their hearts were filled with dread!
They yowled and barked and whimpered,
and as their panic spread,

from Doggy Lodge they bolted
and spewed across the land.
Some rushed into the pampas.
Some trekked across the sand.

Some raced into the forest.
Some drove across the plain.

Some ran into the jungle
or crossed the raging main.

Some taxied through the city
or braved suburban sprawl.

Some blasted into outer space.
Some went not far at all.

Well, ever since that dread event,
what doggies want to know,

even though they *seem* content, is:
"Where'd MY wagger go?"

And that's the reason why, sir,
whenever two dogs meet...

And that's the reason why, ma'am,
in park or yard or street...

And that's the reason why, my child,
before he'll sniff a bone...

a dog will sniff a wagger,
'cause it just might be his own!